ELKHART LAKE PUBLIC LIBRARY
40 Pine Street
P.O. Box R
Elkhart Lake, WI 53020

Earth Day

Written by Margaret McNamara
Illustrated by Mike Gordon

Ready-to-Read
Aladdin Paperbacks
New York   London   Toronto   Sydney

For Don and Arlene Matzkin
—M. M.

ALADDIN PAPERBACKS
An imprint of Simon & Schuster Children's Publishing Division
1230 Avenue of the Americas, New York, NY 10020
Text copyright © 2009 by Margaret McNamara
Illustrations copyright © 2009 by Mike Gordon
All rights reserved, including the right of reproduction in whole or in part in any form.
ALADDIN PAPERBACKS and related logo and READY-TO-READ are
registered trademarks of Simon & Schuster, Inc.
Designed by Sammy Yuen Jr.
The text of this book was set in Century Schoolbook BT.
Manufactured in the United States of America
First Aladdin Paperbacks edition March 2009
2 4 6 8 10 9 7 5 3 1
Library of Congress Cataloging-in-Publication Data
McNamara, Margaret.
Earth Day / by Margaret McNamara; illustrated by Mike Gordon.—
1st Aladdin Paperbacks ed.
p. cm.
(Robin Hill School) (Ready-to-read)
Summary: When Mrs. Connor's class celebrates Earth Day, Emma decides
to start small by recycling, using only what she needs, and picking up
trash when she goes for a walk.
ISBN-13: 978-1-4169-5535-1
ISBN-10: 1-4169-5535-6
[1. Earth Day—Fiction. 2. Environmental protection—Fiction.
3. Schools—Fiction.]
I. Gordon, Mike, ill. II. Title.
PZ7.M47879343Eb 2009
[E]—dc22
2008045418

Earth Day was coming.

The banners in
Mrs. Connor's classroom
read SAVE THE EARTH!

But Emma
did not know how.

The other first graders
had lots of ideas.

"I will rescue
the polar bears!"
said Eigen.

"I will plant a forest!"
said Katie.

"I will save the dolphins!"
said Michael.

"Those are big ideas,"
said Mrs. Connor.

"What other ideas
can you think of?"

When Emma went home,
she was sad.

"I cannot save the Earth,"
Emma said to her dad.
"I do not have any big ideas."

"We can start small,"
said her dad.

"Small is no good,"
said Emma.

"Small is fine," said her dad.

All that week,
Emma and her dad
did small things
to help the Earth.

They shopped at
the farmers market.

Emma brushed her teeth
without running the water.

Her dad turned off the TV.

They went for walks
and picked up trash
along the way.

They sorted cans and bottles.

They used their bikes
instead of the car.

On Earth Day,
Eigen drew a picture
of polar bears.

Katie talked about forests.

Michael made dolphin
noises.

Emma thought about
all the things she did
with her dad.

Emma's small ideas

Then she made her list.

Her list was not long.

From then on,
Mrs. Connor's class
slowed down.

They recycled. And they only used what they needed to.

"Emma's small ideas
are pretty big,"
said Mrs. Connor.

"The Earth is safe
in your hands."